POLKA-DOT PUPPY'S VISITOR

a book about opposites

by Janet Riehecky
illustrated by Linda Hohag

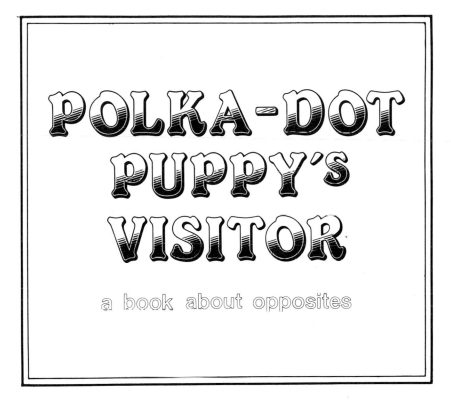

Created by

THE CHILD'S WORLD

Distributed by CHILDREN'S PRESS
Chicago, Illinois

CHILDRENS PRESS HARDCOVER EDITION
ISBN 0-516-05607-7

CHILDRENS PRESS PAPERBACK EDITION
ISBN 0-516-45607-5

Library of Congress Cataloging in Publication Data

Riehecky, Janet, 1953-
    Polka-Dot Puppy's visitor : a book about opposites / by Janet
Riehecky ; illustrated by Linda Hohag.
        p. cm.
    Summary: Everything Polka-Dot Puppy wants to do, Cousin
Petey wants to do the opposite.
    ISBN 0-89565-378-8
    [1. English Language—Synonyms and antonyms—Fiction.
2. Dogs—Fiction.]   I. Hohag, Linda, ill.   II. Title.
PZ7.R4277Po   1988
[E]—dc19   88-10935
                                                    CIP
                                                    AC

1 2 3 4 5 6 7 8 9 10 11 12 R 96 95 94 93 92 91 90 89 88

POLKA-DOT PUPPY'S VISITOR

a book about opposites

Polka-Dot Puppy was very
happy that his cousin,
Petey, had come to visit.

"I am glad you are here, Petey," said Polka-Dot Puppy.

"We can do things together.
Today let's stay inside and
play hide-and-seek."

"I would rather go outside," said Petey.

"Then we will," said Polka-Dot
Puppy. "We can go to the park."

And off they went.

"Let's run as fast as we can,"
said Polka-Dot Puppy.

"I would rather walk nice and slow," said Petey.

"Do we have to go far?" Petey
asked.

"Oh, no," said Polka-Dot Puppy.
"The park is near."

Polka-Dot Puppy climbed up on
the wall. "Come on up, Petey,"
he called.

"I would rather stay down," said
Petey.
"Well, then," said Polka-Dot Puppy.
"Let's do something else together.
We can . . .

jump over the branches."

"I would rather crawl under them."

"We can run to the top of the hill."

"I would rather stay at the bottom."

"We can get wet in the pond."

"I would rather stay dry."

"We can walk on the fence."

"I would rather stay off."

"We can go—" started Polka-Dot
Puppy. But Petey raised his paw.

"I would rather stop," said Petey.
"All right," said Polka-Dot Puppy.

Polka-Dot Puppy and Petey
walked slowly back to the
firehouse.

When they got there, Polka-
Dot Puppy sniffed the air. "I
smell something," he said,
wagging his tail.

"Let's go in the back door."
"I would rather go in the
front," said Petey.

"Oh, come on," said Polka-
Dot Puppy. "I know one
thing we can do together."

Polka-Dot Puppy led the way into
the kitchen. "We can make these
full bowls, empty bowls," he said.

And for once Petey agreed.